Sunrise Summer

MATTHEW SWANSON AND ROBBI BEHR

NEW YORK

It's summer again,
my favorite time of year.

Some families pack swimsuits and sandals when they go on vacation. Mine packs onions and potatoes.

Also doorknobs.

And batteries.

And spark plugs for a Ford 150.

Our trip takes two days
and four flights and
four thousand miles.

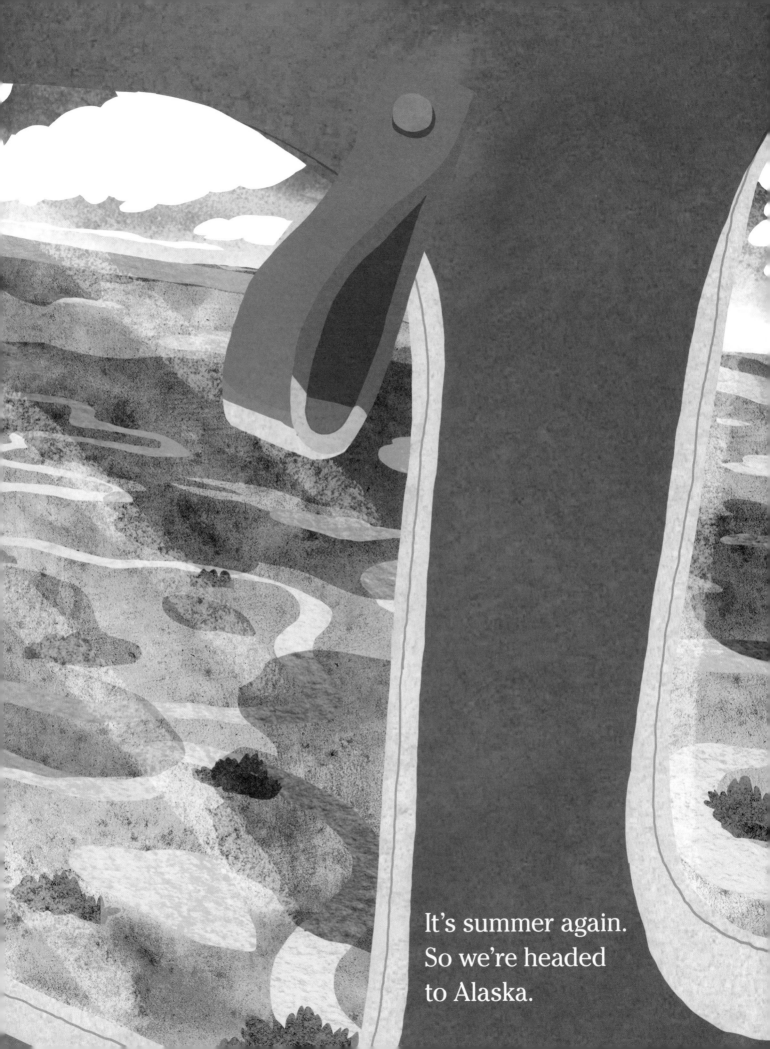

It's summer again.
So we're headed
to Alaska.

Some beaches have boardwalks and
lifeguards and smooth white sand.
Our beach has pebbles and mud
and upside-down jellyfish.

I use a stick to turn
them upside up.

Last summer, I picked tundra berries and made forts in Mole Kingdom.
Last summer, I sat in the truck bed, watching the fishing crew fish.

This summer, I will
join the fishing crew.

While my brothers chase lemmings on the tundra.

And leap from rusted truck beds on the bluff.

And search for agates at the waterline.

I will help twist six-foot anchor poles into the sand.

I will drag endless ropes through knee-deep mud.

I will fetch water from the spring at Coffee Point.

Mama says she thinks the fish are coming soon.
Auntie Maiko says she saw belugas at high tide.
Uncle Roji says, "Who wants a chocolate bar?"

People on the fishing crew
get chocolate bars.

Mama and I catch a ride across the river
to check the mail in Egegik.

One hundred six people live there in the winter, when the
fish are out to sea and it's only light three hours a day.

In summer, the streets are full of people who come from far away to catch the fish and ship them somewhere else.

Mama and I keep an eye on the river,
waiting for the salmon to come.

Until they come, we keep busy.

Mending the nets.

Repainting the outhouse.

Making a pie to thank Kody for fixing our truck.

Then card games.

Then we listen to
the fish report.

The salmon
are coming, it says.

We rush to the window.
The salmon are here.

Mama and I keep an eye on the moon.
The moon shapes the tides. The tides say when we fish.

The tides say that we'll fish at 4:00 AM.

The alarm goes off at 2:30 AM,
but my brothers keep on sleeping.
Breakfast is hot chocolate and cold curry rice.

The fishing crew wears rubber waders.
And special gloves that come up past our elbows.
And woolly hats. Even though it's June.

We keep an eye out for grizzlies, who sleep all day and prowl the beach at night.

We start by stacking the nets. It's raining, but we don't even notice.

We like it when the wind whips.

We don't get nervous
when the waves are high.

We're here to fish.
It's what we do.

At 4:00 AM sharp, Auntie Maiko gives the signal. Uncle Roji pulls his raft into the waves. Mama drives the truck, which drags the net into the water.

My job is tying the net to the rope. I've practiced and practiced the knot.

That's why there is a fishing crew.

The net fills up with fish.
We pick the salmon out by hand.

They're heavy and they're slimy and I need both hands to throw them in the tote.

I drive them to the buyer,
and no one says I shouldn't or I can't.

The rules are different here.

Just like everything else.

Mama and I eat cold spaghetti on the bluff while rain blows sideways up our noses.

It's what we do.

Some people never get to see the sun rise over Bristol Bay. Some people don't get a second chance to tie their first knot.

Some people never get to join the fishing crew.

Those people are not me.

Hello! I'm Robbi.

I drew the pictures for this book. My husband, Matthew, wrote the words. Our children—Alden, Kato, August and Jasper—are the kids you met in this book.

MATTHEW

ALDEN

AUGUST

KATO

JASPER

When I was two, my parents bought a piece of land in a place called Coffee Point, a bump in the tundra at the mouth of the Egegik River, as part of a commercial salmon fishing venture.

They had never fished before. They had never even been to Alaska. But they were looking for adventure and a fun way for our family to spend the summer together. They got plenty of both!

MY BROTHER (UNCLE ROJI)

ME!

MY MOM

MY SISTER (AUNTIE MAIKO!)

(MY DAD WAS TAKING THE PHOTO. NO SELFIE STICKS IN THOSE DAYS!)

Our part of Alaska is very remote.

No roads lead to Coffee Point. To get there, we fly in a jet from Anchorage to King Salmon and then charter a tiny bush plane across the tundra to the beach in front of our cabin.

ALASKA!

CANADA

BRISTOL BAY

COFFEE POINT

KING SALMON

ANCHORAGE

EGEGIK

GULF of ALASKA

There are no stores at Coffee Point, which is why we bring fresh fruit and vegetables with us. Anything that won't fit in our coolers has to be shipped on a barge from Seattle.

There are no paved roads in Coffee Point. No public water. No electric grid. The beach is our highway. We use an empty jug and a plastic tube to collect fresh water from a spring. We gather power from the wind and sun. We have to be resourceful and creative in solving any problems we run into.

There's a hole in the truck's engine!

The four-wheeler won't start!

There's a porcupine in the garage, and it pooped all over everything!

Sorry not sorry.

We also ask for help when we need it. Which is all the time.

I'll just patch it with fiberglass!

Here's how you clean a carburetor!

Trap it in a garbage can and drive it out into the tundra and make sure to leave it in a patch of bushes!

People take care of each other up there.

We fish for sockeye salmon, which hatch in narrow streams and swim across a massive lake and down a river and out to the ocean. A few years later, they are all grown up and come back to lay their eggs in the exact same stream where they hatched. (Amazing!)

The fish follow the same path traveled by the Alaska Natives who have relied on the salmon for centuries. The village of Egegik (right across the river from Coffee Point) was the summer fishing camp for the Aleut people, who kayaked (or walked!) the 70 miles from their winter home of Kanatak.

LAKE BECHAROF

Some of their descendants still live in Egegik, continuing the traditional lifestyle by catching fish, hunting and trapping, and gathering berries and wild greens.

Alaska Natives still catch, dry, smoke, and freeze as many salmon as they need for eating over the winter. But most of the fishermen (including us) are catching fish to sell—as a business. The salmon are a precious (and valuable!) natural resource. In order to keep the river system from being overfished, people are not allowed to catch salmon without a special permit. (We have three.)

MY PERMIT

OUR RADIO (old school!)

Four times a day throughout the summer fishing season, biologists who work for the Alaska Department of Fish and Game broadcast a fish report that tells us how many salmon have made it up the river to lay their eggs.

By keeping track of the number of fish that lay their eggs this year, the Fish and Game scientists make sure there will be plenty of salmon coming back next year, and all the years after that. There are strict rules about what time we can put our nets in the water and when we have to take them back out. Once enough fish have made it up the river, the biologists let us fish.

CORKLINE
CORKS (they float!)
10 feet deep
GILLS
(like the metal)
LEADLINE (so heavy!)

The nets we use to fish are called gill nets, because the salmon swim into them and get caught around their gills.

We are "set-net" fishermen, which means we do our fishing from the shore, where the nets are "set" in place.

We create a huge rectangle of rope with anchors and pulleys at each corner and attach our nets to the rope. At the exact second that the Department of Fish and Game says we're allowed to begin, we use our trucks to drag the nets into the water. And then we cross our fingers that there are fish!

There are also "drifters" who fish farther from the shore and pull their nets behind them in boats.

PULLEY
ANCHOR
BEACH
NET
RIVER
BUOY
PULLEY
"DRIFTER"

Once our nets are in the water, we wait for them to fill up with fish. Then we pull ourselves along the net in a small rubber raft and remove each salmon by hand.

As soon as the raft is full, we sell the salmon to people in large trucks (with cranes that lift and weigh our fish), who drive them up the beach to a processing plant where they are cut into fillets, frozen, and shipped all over the world.

1. Pick fish out of net.

2. Sell the fish.

3. Fish get processed on the "SLIME LINE."

4. Fish are shipped all over the world. Makes great sushi!　おいしい!

In an average summer, our family catches about ten thousand fish—not including the ones we eat!

We are so grateful that we get to spend our summers in this magical place and so pleased to share a tiny bit of it with you.

If you ever find yourself in our distant corner of Alaska, please stop by and fix our truck, and we'll gladly bake you a pie.

To our friends and neighbors at Coffee Point: Gratitude, good luck, and good fishing.

With thanks to Jessica Chernikoff and the Egegik Village Council.

[Imprint]
MAKE YOUR MARK

A part of Macmillan Publishing Group, LLC
120 Broadway, New York, NY 10271

ABOUT THIS BOOK

The characters for this book were drawn by hand with pen and ink and gouache on Arches hot-pressed watercolor paper. The backgrounds are digital collage of sampled watercolor washes done in Adobe Photoshop using a Cintiq 13 HD Tablet. The text was set in ITC Cheltenham, and the display type is Proprietor Roman. The book was edited by Erin Stein and designed by Natalie C. Sousa. The production was supervised by Raymond Colón and the production editor was Dawn Ryan.

SUNRISE SUMMER. Text copyright © 2020 by Matthew Swanson. Illustrations copyright © 2020 by Robbi Behr. All rights reserved. Printed in China by Toppan Leefung Printing Ltd., Dongguan City, Guangdong Province.

Library of Congress Cataloging-in-Publication Data
Names: Swanson, Matthew, 1974– author. | Behr, Robbi, illustrator.
Title: Sunrise summer / Matthew Swanson and Robbi Behr.
Description: First edition. | New York : Imprint, 2020. | Audience: Ages 4–7. | Audience: Grades K–1. |
Summary: Each summer, a young girl and her family travel to remote Egegik, Alaska, where they join a salmon fishing crew.
Identifiers: LCCN 2019036930 | ISBN 9781250080585 (hardcover)
Subjects: CYAC: Summer—Fiction. | Vacations—Fiction. | Family life—Alaska—Fiction | Salmon fishing—Fiction. | Alaska—Fiction
Classification: LCC PZ7.S9719 Su 2020 | DDC [E]—dc23
LC record available at https://lccn.loc.gov/2019036930

Our books may be purchased in bulk for promotional, educational, or business use. Please contact your local bookseller or the Macmillan Corporate and Premium Sales Department at (800) 221-7945 ext. 5442 or by email at MacmillanSpecialMarkets@macmillan.com.

Imprint logo designed by Amanda Spielman

First edition, 2020

1 3 5 7 9 10 8 6 4 2

mackids.com

This book is here for your reaction.
(We hope, of course, for satisfaction.)
But when you're done, don't try to steal it,
Or cursed you'll be. (You're sure to feel it.)
For truly, if we get our wish,
You'll smell an awful lot like fish.